The Tower & The Flower

D1501408

To all the Twinses,
    You are blessings
all of you!
    Blessings,

Nancy De Graw McSwane

The Tower & The Flower

Nancy DeGraw McSwane
Illustrated by Danielle Malmet Rodger

Xulon Press Elite
2301 Lucien Way #415
Maitland, FL 32751
407.339.4217
www.xulonpress.com

Paperback ISBN-13: 978-1-66281-588-1
Ebook ISBN-13: 978-1-66281-589-8

Acknowledgements:

My thanks first goes to the Creator of all things, His Son and the Holy Spirit.

I also thank the architects of the beautiful Ely Cathedral.

Many thanks goes to my husband and my two beloved daughters as well as my beautiful granddaughter. I am also thankful and could not have done this book without the inspired watercolors of Danielle Malmet Rodger, the graphic work by my son Dillon McSwane, and the organizational input by my son Dustin McSwane.

Also untold thanks to the loving generous family that sent my husband and I on a wonderful vacation in England. We have not been the same since the trip.

And last but not least, thanks to John and Lois Lakeman for the teachings that encouraged me to finish what I believed God had placed in my heart, publishing this little poem.

I once sat on a bench, I had some time to spare,

And there I heard two voices fill the morning air.

I listened to them speaking, the voices deep and fine,

Were debating concerning the divine.

Walking to the garden, to hear more from the two,

I first saw a violet shimmering in the dew.

And then I saw a tower. I was confused and surprised.
I saw no one else as I blinked my wondering eyes,

The church above was speaking or so it seemed to me
And the flower below was asking for the church's company.

Said the violet to the tower, "I love to hear you sing."

Rang the tower to the flower," "What you say doesn't mean a thing."

Don't you see that you are small, your opinion doesn't matter at all.

How dare you deem us to be the same,

My creator was obviously pleased with me

But you should be ashamed.

I am *grand*,

and stand above the rooftops

But you are low and barely show among
the common crops.

Do you know my famous history?
Have you seen my *lofty* walls?

You haven't ever visited me or bowed
in my *arched* halls.

But softly said the flower, daring again to speak

Haven't you heard your preacher's preach,

"Blessed are the meek."

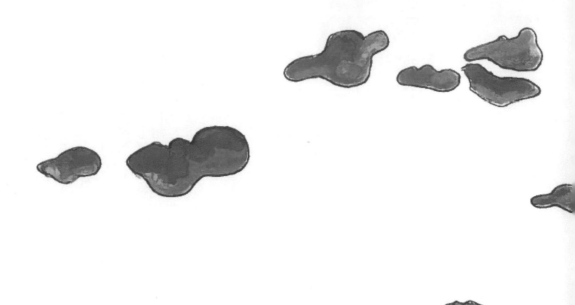

You see I serve and work in ways you can never do.

We were both planted here for reasons that are true.

In seasons the farmer took me and had my seedlings sown

By country streets and garden walls, my faithful seeds were blown

And you, you were built by man, as grand as grand can be.

So both of us were made for joy, Oh sweet mystery.

I heard a throaty bong but words I did not hear

And the flower seemed to grow larger in the shadow of her peer.

The Cathedral showing beauty as did the violets design

So thoughtfully I walked away from the dialogue divine.

Authors notes:

Ely Cathedral was founded in 673 AD by the daughter of the East Anglican king in the town of Cambridgeshire, England. Her name was Etheldreda. Isn't that a great name for a princess? In 970 the Vikings came and overran the abbey and did what Vikings of that day did, killed a lot of clergy and tore down buildings. The Vikings became Christian and were called Normans. The Normans started to reconstruct the Cathedral in 1083. That means it is 1,348 years old.

Ely Cathedral has remained a place of Christian worship during many wars. Some English soldiers tore down many of Ely's statues. Some of its beautiful stained glass is gone too. However, it still stands today. I enjoyed singing in the beautiful Cathedral when I went to visit.

It is overwhelming. The enormous size of the nave can make a mere person feel very small. I walked outside because I felt so insignificant in that awesome building and I saw a violet.

Violets and their species are said to be 13 thousand years old. That's a lot older than Ely Cathedral.

Violets are maybe 6 inches tall. Ely Cathedral at its tallest point is 217 feet. It is so tall and beautiful as the violet is so small but just as beautiful, in a different way.

And that is what this poem is about. We can be small like the little children that this poem is read to, or as tall and mighty as Ely Cathedral. We can be seemingly insignificant as a small flower, but we all have an important job to do in showing God's glory.

CPSIA information can be obtained
at www.ICGtesting.com
Printed in the USA
BVHW060243280621
610410BV00001B/1